T0129083

Betsy's Dream

EDNA NEWBURY

Order this book online at www.trafford.com
or email orders@trafford.com

Most Trafford titles are also available at major online book retailers.

© Copyright 2012 Edna Newbury.
All rights reserved. No part of this publication may be reproduced, stored in a retrieval system,
or transmitted, in any form or by any means, electronic, mechanical, photocopying, recording,
or otherwise, without the written prior permission of the author.

Printed in the United States of America.

ISBN: 978-1-4669-6518-8 (sc)
ISBN: 978-1-4669-6517-1 (e)

Trafford rev. 10/22/2012

 www.trafford.com

North America & international
toll-free: 1 888 232 4444 (USA & Canada)
phone: 250 383 6864 ♦ fax: 812 355 4082

It was a hot day in September when Betsy just arrived home from school. Betsy lived in the city with her mother and father. She never had any sisters or brothers. She was a only child. Betsy had lots of friends at school. Her best friend Sally had just moved away and that made Betsy really sad.

But Betsy didn't expect to come from school and find that there were strangers in the house waiting for her. There were two social workers and a police woman waiting inside for her to return home from school. Betsy's neighbour Mrs. Lee was also there and she was crying. Mrs. Lee was staying wuth Betsy while her parents were away on a business trip. Mrs. Lee sat Betsy down and explained to her that her parents were killed in a plane crash while returning home.

Betsy was stunned, she couldn't believe what she was hearing, she was shocked and she didn't know what she was going to do. Betsy ran into her bedroom. Mrs. Lee ran after her and told her that she was going to be just fine. Betsy trusted Mrs. Lee and she believed what she was saying. She knew she was going to be ok. Betsy wanted to be alone for a few minutes just to think. Mrs. Lee told Betsy that her aunt Elaine was coming to pick her up. Betsy was a little nervous at that thought because she had never met her aunt. Betsy knew she had a aunt Elaine and that she was her mother's sister.

A few days had passed and after the funerals of Betsy's parents her aunt Elaine arrived at the house with a loading van. Betsy was told that her aunt Elaine was very pretty. It seems that there was a huge disagreement between the two sisters and they never kept in touch.

Betsy opened the front door when her aunt knocked. Betsy couldn't believe her eyes. She thought she was looking at her mother. She thought they could have been twins, they were so much alike. But that was impossible because she was ten years younger then Betsy's mother. It was just for a moment then Betsy realized who she was. It was just wishful thinking on her part. Aunt Elaine asked Betsy if she could come in and Betsy said yes.

They both went inside and started talking. They talked for hours. Before they realized the time it was getting late and they both were so tired.

Betsy's questions were all answered. Aunt Elaine asked Betsy if she would like to come and live with her on her ranch. Betsy agreed that it would be a good idea to go and live with her aunt instead of going to live with strangers.

Betsy asked her aunt Elaine where she lived and what she did for a living. Her aunt told her that she owned a ranch and that she raised horses.

When Betsy heard this her eyes lit up like diamonds she got so excited. Betsy loved horses and she always wanted to be in the Nationals as an equestrian rider. Betsy always dreamed of jumping over posts and logs on a beautiful horse.

What Betsy didn't know was that all of her dreams were about to come true. It took a few hours to get all of her stuff packed up and loaded into the moving van. But finally they got everything packed away in the van. Betsy said good-bye to Mrs. Lee and told her that she would be just fine and that she would write as soon as she gets settled at her new home. Betsy took one final look at her home that she was leaving for good. In no time they were on their way. While they were driving aunt Elaine was telling Betsy all about her ranch. She told Betsy she had a surprise for her when they get there. Betsy could hardly wait to get there. All because there were horses on the big ranch.

It took them fifteen hours to get to the ranch but they finally arrived there. Betsy could hardly believe her eyes. The ranch was so beautiful. It was almost like a fairy tale coming true for her. There were horses everywhere and the hills were a marvellous green, it was just breath taking. The hills were as far as the eyes could see. The ranch was big and beautiful.

Aunt Elaine and Betsy carried all of her things into the ranch house. A couple of ranch hands helped them. Her aunt told her that she could choose any room in the house. Betsy chose the room with the big bay window so she could watch the horses running in the fields. When Betsy was all settled away they both had something to eat.

Betsy was wondering what the surprise was that her aunt had for her. She could hardly wait to see what it was. She thought it was something in a small box or something. But aunt Elaine never gave her a small box or anything, all she said was to follow her outside for a minute. When they got outside aunt Elaine showed her some horses over in the field that she was trying to tame. Betsy's aunt told her to choose any horse that she wanted for her very own. Betsy couldn't believe what she was hearing. Her aunt had just given her something that she always wanted. Something that she always dreamed of having. Betsy didn't know what to say she was so speechless. Betsy saw a shy white horse in the corner of the field. That was the one that she wanted. It seemed like they had something in common. It was as if they were meant to be together.

Betsy called to the horse and the horse came right up to her. As if though they knew each other all their lives. Betsy named her horse Blazing Snow. That name seemed to be fitting for the horse because the horse was as pure white as the new fallen snow and its coat glistened in the sunlight. When all the excitement was over Betsy gave aunt Elaine the biggest kiss and hug that she had ever given anyone in her life. Betsy gave her new horse Blazing Snow a kiss on the head. Betsy thanked her aunt and promised her that she would always take care of it. Aunt Elaine and Betsy went back inside, it was drawing close to supper time.

When they had finished eating and the dishes were all cleaned up and put away they looked around to make sure everything was all taken care of and cleaned away for the night. For that was one thing that aunt Elaine hated an untidy house.

It was getting late so they got ready for bed. Betsy gave her aunt a kiss good-night and thanked her again for everything and especially for taking her in instead of sending her to an orphanage. Aunt Elaine told her that she would never dream of sending her away. Family meant everything to her.

They bid their farewells good-night and they both went to bed.

It didn't seem like anytime had past when Betsy awoke the next morning. When Betsy got out of bed she fell to her knees and thanked God for sending her aunt to her and for taking care of her.

When she had finished saying her prayers she got dressed and went downstairs. The smells were like a fresh morning breeze. Aunt Elaine was cooking breakfast. It smelled and tasted delicious.

It was time for Betsy to get ready for her first day of school. She was a little nervous. Aunt Elaine bought her everything she needed for school.

They walked out to the bus stop together. Betsy's new school was five miles away so she had to travel by bus. But, she didn't mind that. When they arrived at the bus stop aunt Elaine wished her a good day and told her that she would see her after school. The bus finally arrived and when it came to a stop Betsy stepped inside the bus. Everyone on the bus just stared at her. They didn't know there was going to be a new girl at their school.

Betsy walked to the back of the bus. There was a girl sitting by herself. The girl told Betsy that her name was Jill. The two girls were the same age and were about the same growth. They hit it of perfectly. Everyone smiled at Betsy they all seemed so nice on the bus. Jill told all of them that her name was Betsy and they all said hi to her. Even the bus driver introduced himself, his name was Jack Day.

Betsy couldn't wait to get to her new school to see what it was like. She figured it was going to be a lot different then her old school. Finally the bus arrived at the school and Betsy was right it was so much smaller then her old school. But she didn't care, it was going to be her school too. At school Jill introduced Betsy to all her friends. Everyone all seemed to be so friendly. The school bell rang and everyone went to their classrooms. When all the students were seated to their desks the teacher asked Betsy to come up to the front of the class to tell everyone who she was.

Betsy did has the teacher asked and went to the front of the class. Betsy told them where she had come front and why she had come to live with her aunt on her ranch. Betsy didn't know just how famous her aunt was until much later. The teacher thanked Betsy for telling them all about herself.

Then the teacher went around the classroom and asked everyone to tell Betsy their names as well.

All of her new classmates seemed all so nice and friendly. They were not much like the people back in her old school. Back there it seemed that if you were not in the in-crowd then you weren't anyone important. But at this school everyone seemed to like each other. And that was just fine with Betsy.

The teacher's name was Mr. Mahoney and he was very nice.

When school was over they all went home for the day. Betsy asked Jill if she would like to come to the ranch with her and Jill said that she would love to. When the school bus reached the ranch aunt Elaine was waiting at the end of the lane for Betsy. Betsy introduced Jill to her aunt. They both said hi to each other at the same time. While they were walking towards the ranch house it started to rain. Aunt Elaine asked Jill if she would like to join them for dinner. Jill said that she would love to stay and it was ok with her but she had to call her mother and ask if it was ok to stay for dinner.

When they reached the ranch house Jill was so amazed by its beauty. They all went inside the house. Jill called her mother on the phone and asked if it was okay if she could stay at the ranch house with her new friend for dinner. Jill told her mother that Betsy and her aunt would give her a ride home after dinner. Her mother told her that it would be fine with her.

Jill lived a mile down the road from the ranch house. She always wanted to know what the ranch house looked like inside and now she finally she knew. Jill told aunt Elaine that her house was beautiful. Aunt Elaine said thank-you and told her that she was welcomed there at anytime. After dinner Betsy took Jill out into the stables to see the horse that her aunt had given to her. Jill was amazed at how beautiful the horse was. Betsy told Jill she was going to train Blazing Snow for the Nationals and that she wanted to be an a equestrian rider.

It was getting late and it was almost time for Jill to be getting home. Betsy and her aunt drove Jill home. It was still raining outside. Before Jill reached her house she thanked them both for a great time and for dinner. The longer Betsy stayed with her aunt the more she grew to love her. Sometimes Betsy rode on the bus and other times she would ride Blazing Snow to school. When she rode her horse to school she would put her in the nearby stable until school was over. Jill lived near town but on weekends the came out to the ranch with Betsy. They had so much fun together. Jill was like the sister that Betsy never had. They spent all the time they could together.

During summer break Jill would come over out to the ranch and spent all her time there helping Betsy train for the horse back jumping contests.

Betsy was in a lot of races and contests with Blazing Snow and won just about most of them. But winning the nationals was a life long dream for Betsy. Betsy had just turned sixteen when her dreams were just about to come true. The Nationals were going to be held in town. Betsy and Jill gave Blazing Snow a good grooming. Blazing Snow's coat glistened in the sunlight, she was such a beautiful horse. Jumping over posts and logs were Blazing Snow's favourite things to do.

Betsy and her horse were training for a long time.

They could hardly wait for their special day to come.

When the day had finally arrived for Betsy to ride Blazing Snow in the Nationals something wonderful happened. Aunt Elaine brought Betsy's grandmother to the Nationals to see Betsy race.

Betsy could hardly believe her eyes when she saw her. She didn't know that aunt Elaine was going to bring her grandmother there. Betsy was so happy everything was going really swell for her. All the riders took their turns jumping over the posts.

When it was time for Betsy's turn she was so excited. The gun went off and Blazing Snow took of like lightning. She jumped over every post perfectly and everyone was clapping and cheering like crazy. When they had finished the solemn everyone jumped out of their seats and gave them a standing ovation. Betsy could hardly believe that she had finally did it. The judges were calling out the scores and Betsy had won the Nationals with a perfect score.

She could hardly believe it, her dream had finally come true, she was the champion. Betsy didn't do it for the money, she did it for her parents.

Her grandmother and aunt Elaine were so overwhelmed that they could hardly believe it. They always knew that Betsy could do it. Her Grandmother told her that her parents would have been So proud of her. Although her parents were not there in body she knew they were there in spirit.

It felt a sif they were her guardian angels looking down on her. Betsy could feel their presence around her. Betsy knew that her parents were there in her heart. After the Nationals were over aunt Elaine invited all of Betsy's friends to come out to the ranch for a big celebration. Jill was so proud of Betsy. Her very best friend was a champion equestrian rider. At the age of sixteen that was a great accomplishment. At the party all of Betsy's friends were there from school. Everyone was having such a great time. Betsy was the youngest female rider that ever entered the Nationals and won. It was a great feeling to achieve that goal in such a early life.

Everyone on the ranch gave Betsy gifts and money she was so happy. The money that everyone had given to her she had decided to put it into a bank account for college. She always promised her parents that she would go to college.

There was dancing and lots of laughter at the party.

When the party was starting to die down, Betsy thanked everyone for the gifts and the party. She also thanked everyone for coming. Betsy and Jill bid their good-night to the crowd and went inside the house and went upstairs to her room. Jill was so proud of Betsy, and she was also so excited for her. Jill wanted to be a doctor when she got out of school. Betsy knew that Jill would be a terrific doctor because she was really good with people. Jill knew things about medicine that Betsy could never understand. All Betsy dreamed about was horses and a real good man, someone who would treat her well. She wanted someone like her father. She knew that a man like that was going to be hard to find because when God made he father he broke the mold. Hopefully there was someone special out there for her. Betsy had plenty of time to look for that special someone, she had he whole life ahead of her. She never had any intentions of getting mixed up with anyone right now.

The summer was coming to an end. It had been a really terrific summer. She had achieved a lot of good things in her life this past summer. She had made a lot of new friends at the Nationals and new friends on the rance when people came to ride the horses. Aunt Elaine donated her time and horses to a orphanage for kids that didn't have any families to take care of them. Most of the children lost their parents in accidents or they got killed some other way. Betsy knew how they felt losing their parents. But, she had someone to take care of her and love her. And she was very thankful and grateful for that. She loved her grandmother and aunt Elaine so much. She didn't know how she could repay them. But they didn't want to be repaid. All they wanted was her love and they got plenty of that.

The first day of school had finally arrived and Betsy was so excited. She could hardly wait to see all her friends again. The school bus stopped outside the ranch gate as usual but something seemed to be different. When Betsy stepped onto the bus everyone started to clap for her. They were all so happy for her. They also wanted her autograph and Betsy felt so proud to have so many good friends. When she went to sit her usual seat there was someone new sitting there. It was a guy that Betsy could not keep her eyes off, he was so good looking. He had jet black hair and deep green eyes He was absolutely gorgeous. His name was Joey, he seemed to be a little shy. Joey said his to her but it was so low that Betsy wasn't sure if he had said hi to her or it was something else. So Betsy decided to say hi back to him. After that he started to speak to her. All the way to the school on the bus they talked and all the way to the school doors they talked. It was as if they were the only two people there. They even sat together for lunch. Jill sat with them and a few more friends joined them for lunch. It was as if God had answered her prayers and sent her an angel from heaven. They talked like they were two old friend s trying to catch up on old news. Jill told Betsy that they seemed to be a real good match. Betsy blushed because she knew that Joey was her very first crush. But, Betsy knew that at first sight that she really liked Joey. A few months had passed and the schools first dance was coming up. Jill was asked by a nice guy in her class to go to the dance. And of course Betsy was asked by none other then Joey.

She was so excited about the dance because this was going to be the first dance that she had ever been too. It was going to be very special for her. Jill and Betsy went to the mall looking for their dresses. Betsy had picked out her dress that she wanted and it was beautiful. There was this one dress that Jill really liked but she never had enough to buy it. Betsy wanted to buy it for her. Jill couldn't except it but Betsy insisted that she take it for being such a good friend. Betsy told Jill that she was more like a sister then a friend. So Jill didn't know how she could say no to that.

When all tears of joy had finished falling and they were all dried off they went to try on their dresses. The dresses fit them both perfectly. Betsy paid for both of the dresses and they headed home. Aunt Elaine thought the dresses were absolutely beautiful. The night of the dance had finally arrived. Joey picked up Betsy in a white limousine. When they got to the limo he told her how beautiful she looked. Then he gave her a blue corsage and a stunning sapphire pendant. It both matched her dress perfectly. Joey didn't have any idea that Betsy was wearing a blue dress. It was as if they had the same track mind. Joey and Betsy met Jill and her date at the dance. Betsy told Jill that she looked radiant. Everyone thought Betsy looked beautiful. Betsy thought ut was a school dance but it wasn't. It was a surprise party for Betsy It seemed that everyone wanted to give her a party.

They all thought Betsy was a true champion and that she was their champion. When Betsy and Joey walked into the gymnasium everyone clapped and cheered for her, she didn't know what to say. For once she was speechless. She turned to Joey and hugged him so tight that he could hardly breathe.

The principal Mr. Hale went to the podium and asked Betsy if she would please come up on stage.

All the while she was walking up on stage with Joey by her side she was crying. She couldn't believe that everyone had did something like this for her. Mr. Hale presented Betsy with a present from the whole school. She opened it and it was a beautiful gold broach with a horse filled with diamonds. Betsy thought that it was just lovely. Joey pinned it on her dress. She said thank-you to every one and she started to cry again. Everyone started clapping for her again. The band started to play Betsy's favourite song. It was "from this moment".

Mr. Hale asked Betsy and Joey if they would start the first dance of the night. When they started to dance she felt so loved. Betsy and Joey looked so peaceful while they were dancing. It was a wonderful party and Betsy asked Joey how the band knew what her favourite song was. He told her that he had told them. He didn't think she would mind and she didn't. She thought that it was a very special thing to do. When the band had finished playing a huge picture of Betsy winning the Nationals was unveiled. The picture was hanging from the rafters.

Betsy could hardly believe her eyes. Betsy thanked everyone again. The party was starting to die down and everyone was starting to leave. Joey asked Betsy if she wanted to leave. She decided to leave because she was getting a little tired.

When they reached the car Joey got down on one knee and asked Betsy if she would like to go steady with him. It didn't take long for her to say yes.

They kissed and declared their love for eachother.

Joey placed a diamond ring on her finger she told him that it was so beautiful. On the way home Joey sang "from this moment" to Betsy. Betsy started to cry again. Joey told her that she had better get used to it because he loved her so much. She told him that she had a wonderful night and it would be a night that she would never forget. When they reached the ranch Joey walked Betsy to the front door and gave her a long passionate kiss goodnight. When he drove of Betsy ran inside the house. Her aunt Elaine was already gone to bed because it was late. Betsy ran upstairs, got undressed and jumped in a warm refreshing bath. She just sat there in a tub full of bubbles. While she was soaking in the bubbles she phoned Jill and told her everything that happened after she left the party.

Jill was so happy for her when she told her that Joey asked her to go steady. Betsy told Jill that Joey sang to her on the way home in the limo. Jill thought that it was so romantic. Betsy tried to explain to her what the ring looked like. Jill could hardly wait to see the ring. Well, it was getting late so Betsy said good-night to Jill and told her that she would see tomorrow. When Betsy got out of the tub and dried off she went straight to bed. She wasn't in bed long when the phone rang it was Joey calling her to wish her a good-night and he told her that he loved her. She told him she loved him too and then he hung up. It didn't take very long for Betsy to fall asleep.

The next morning Betsy woke up and smelled fresh coffee, bacon and eggs frying. It smelled wonderful so she jumped out of bed, got dressed and ran downstairs. When she sat down to the table aunt Elaine asked her if she could see her ring. Aunt Elaine told Betsy that Joey asked her if it was okay if he asked Betsy to go steady and she told him that it was just fine with her. Aunt Elaine really liked Joey and she thought that he was a kind, sweet and loving person. Joey told aunt Elaine that he loved Betsy more then life itself. That was enough for aunt Elaine to hear. Aunt Elaine told Betsy that her parents would have loved Joey just as much she did. It wasn't long after they had finished eating breakfast when Jill arrived at the ranch. Jill didn't even knock on the door, she was to excited to see Betsy's ring. Jill told Betsy that Joey had good taste in jewelry and he had especially great taste in girlfriends. Betsy told them that she had a wonderful time last night. She was really shocked when she found out that the so called dance was really a party for her. She never realized how many good friends she had until last night.

She was so grateful to have so many good friends.

Betsy couldn't believe there was a picture of her placed in the school gymnasium for everyone to see. Everyone that would come and visit the school to play basketball or volleyball would see her and Blazing Snow hanging in the rafters. Inside she felt so proud of that. Jill could hardly wait to get to school and congratulate Joey for getting promised to her best friend. When Betsy and Jill arrived at school Joey met them at the door. He gave Betsy a good morning kiss. Everyone was looking at them and all Betsy did was blush. No one knew that Betsy and Joey were going steady until some of the girls saw the beautiful ring on Bets's finger. They were so happy for them both. When Betsy went to her locker she found a white rose stuck between the doors and she knew where it came from, Joey just smiled. They all went to their classroom and there was another white rose on her desk. But, this time there was a note with it. It read "From this day forward you will receive a white rose and know that white will never fade just like my love for you", love Joey.

Betsy was so touched that she started to cry.

She gave Joey a kiss and thanked him for loving her so much. All of the girls ha d a little tear in their eyes. They all thought that it was so romantic. The school bell rang and everyone took their seats.

When the teacher came into the classroom she wondered why all the girls were wiping their eyes.

Jill told her what had happened and she thought it was so sweet.

All during class Betsy couldn't keep her eyes of Joey and it seemed that every time she looked at him he was staring back at her. Betsy could hardly concentrate on her work but, she knew she had to.

When school was over for the day Joey walked out with Betsy to his car. He asked if she wanted to ride on the bus or if she would rather ride with him.

And of course she rode with him. All of her friends thought that Joey was an angel in disguise. It was as if he was sent from heaven to Betsy.

On the way home they talked about what they wanted to do when they got out of school. Betsy told Joey that she wanted to be a horse trainer and that she still wanted to ride horses. Joey wanted to be a veterinarian, he always wanted that. They both decided that they would have their own place full of horses and Joey would have his own practise where they lived. They didn't want any children any time soon. Betsy didn't want to put her kids through what she went through just incase anything happened to her. When they arrived at the ranch everything was quiet. There was no one to be seen.

They got out of the car and went inside the house.

Betsy called out to aunt Elaine but there was no answer. She went upstairs and found her aunt on the bedroom floor. Betsy called out to Joey and he ran upstairs and went into the bedroom. He listened to see if he could find a heart beat. Joey found a heart beat but it was really slow and weak. Betsy got up off the floor and went and called the hospital it took awhile for someone to answer the phone.

When someone finally answered the phone Betsy told them that they needed a ambulance as soon as possible. The nurse asked what was wrong.

Betsy told the nurse that he aunt was unconscious.

The nurse told her that the ambulance would be at the ranch as soon as possible. Betsy didn't have any idea what had happened to her aunt. Betsy and Joey stayed with her until the ambulance arrived. When the ambulance drove off Betsy and Joey followed right behind them. It seemed like forever for them to reach the hospital. But, finally they arrived there. By the time they carried aunt Elaine into the hospital she had come to. She had told them that she had been stung by a bumblebee and she was allergic to bees. The doctor kept her in over night just to keep a watch over her.

She was released early the next morning. Betsy and Joey was there at the hospital to pick her up. It was a great relief that she was going to be ok. Betsy told her aunt that she had given her one of the biggest scares that she had ever received in her life. The doctor gave aunt Elaine some medicine to help get down the swelling form the sting. When they arrived back on the ranch Betsy told her aunt to go straight to bed. Betsy walked upstairs and helped her get into bed. While they were upstairs Joey was downstairs making breakfast. He brewed some fresh coffee, french toast, scrambled eggs and bacon. He carried a tray upstairs to aunt Elaine in bed. She thought that it was so sweet of him to do that. She told him that he didn't have to do that but he said he wanted to. She thanked him for the great meal and Joey told her that he loved to cook.

While she was eating her breakfast Betsy and Joey went downstairs and sat together at the table for the very first time alone and ate breakfast together.

Betsy told him that he should become a chef instead of a vet because he was a terrific cook. It seemed a little awkward eating together alone but Joey told her that they would have to get used to it if they planned on being married someday. When they had finished eating Betsy went upstairs and got her aunts tray. She told Betsy that it was one of the best breakfasts that she had ever tasted in a long time. Betsy took the tray downstairs while her aunt took a nap. When Betsy went downstairs Joey had just about all of the dishes and the kitchen cleaned. Betsy felt so lucky to have a fellow that was not afraid to do housework. Joey told Betsy that he loved being in the kitchen cooking and cleaning. He also did other kinds of housework.

Joey said that when it was time for him to move into his own house with his new wife that she wouldn't have to do all the housework. He said that housework wasn't only for women. Betsy gave Joey a long passionate kiss and said thank-you to him for coming into her life. Joey said that he was glad he did as well. Joey was a only child also so he was used to helping his mother around the house.

When all the cleaning was done Betsy and Joey went in the living room and sat on the couch together. Joey asked Betsy if she ever thought about marriage. Betsy told him that she thought about it once in awhile., only if she found the right man.

Joey told Betsy that she didn't have to look any farther because she had already found the right man.

Betsy smiled at Joey an said "maybe I have too".

Joey gave her a kiss and told her that he will love her forever.

Graduating from highschool was drawing near.

Betsy was thinking about all the wonderful times she has had in her highschool years. She had the best friend that anyone could ever ask for and the best boyfriend that any girl could ever have. Everything was just perfect, she remembered when her aunt Elaine had taken her in when her parents were killed. But the best day of all was when she met Joey. Although it was almost seven years it was hard to believe how fast the time as gone and it passed so quickly.

Betsy and Jill went shopping for their graduation gowns. It was taking them awhile to choose the right gown that they wanted. They wanted to find the perfect gown. They couldn't believe that they were going to be apart for the next four years. And Betsy knew that no matter where they all ended up they would be best friends for life. Betsy told Jill that she didn't know what she was going to do without Joey. What Betsy didn't know was that Jill and Joey were accepted to the same college that Betsy was going to. They weren't going to tell Betsy until graduation day. They thought that it would be a great surprise for her. When they finally chose the gowns they wanted they went and paid for them. They went home and hung the gowns in the closet so they wouldn't get all wrinkled. Betsy and Jill went to the stables to get Blazing Snow and another horse to go for a ride. They went over the hills and down through the valley. They stopped and sat by the rivers edge to watch the ducks swimming in the water. It was so beautiful and peaceful there. They talked about all the great times they had together. They also talked about their graduation day and college and what it was going to be like not being around each other for a long time. Betsy told Jill that they were going to see each other for the holidays. Jill found it so hard not to tell Betsy that they were all going to the same college together. Betsy told Jill that she was just like a sister that she always wanted. She told Jill that she loved her and that she was the best friend that anyone could ever ask for. The two girls hugged each other. When the tears had finally stopped they got back on the horses and went back to the ranch. They had returned home just in the nick of time because it started to rain.

Graduation day had finally arrived. Betsy and Jill had gotten dressed together. Jill's gown was gold and Betsy's gown was silver. When they finally finished getting ready they went downstairs. Jill's date and Joey were waiting in the living room for them. The two guys were speechless when they saw the two beautiful girls. Jill's date gave her a dozen red roses and a gold locket. Jill thanked him and told him it was beautiful. Joey gave Betsy a dozen white roses and a silver diamond bracelet.

Betsy kissed him and told him that she loved it. The two couples arrived at the school in a black limousine. The other graduates thought that Jill and Betsy looked so stunning. They all went inside and went straight to the gymnasium. The gym was decorated beautifully. They never saw it look so lovely.

Everyone looked wonderful and it all looked so nice.

Before long the ceremony was about to start.

There were lots of graduates. By the time everything was over they were all starting to get a little restless. They all couldn't wait to get to the dance of their lives. After all it was going to be the last dance that they will ever have in that school. Everything was going perfectly. When the dance was half over Jill and Joey told Betsy that they had something to tell her and it was very important. Jill and Joey never cracked a smile. Betsy didn't know what to expect. Everything was running through Betsy's mind. She didn't know what to think. The three friends all went to one side of the room. Joey asked Betsy if she would please have a seat. Betsy thought that it was something serious. Jill started to laugh and she knew then it wasn't anything very serious.

Joey got down on one knee and asked Betsy if she would marry him. Jill was shocked she didn't know that Joey was going to purpose to Betsy. But, she was so happy for her. Betsy's mouth fell open she was stunned. She didn't know what to say at first. She didn't know if it was better to laugh or cry.

So she did a little of both. Betsy knew that she loved Joey with all of her heart and soul. Finally she yes to Joey. He got up of the floor and placed a diamond ring on her finger. What Betsy didn't realize was that everyone was watching. And after

Joey gave her a kiss the whole gymnasium started to clap and whistle. Everyone was so happy for them.

But now it was Jill's turn to tell Betsy some good news. By this time Betsy was more curious then ever. Getting purposed to was shocking enough but she was so curious at what Jill wanted to say.

Betsy couldn't wait any longer she told Jill to spill it.

And finally Jill told Betsy that herself and Joey was accepted to the same college that she was. Betsy couldn't believe what she was hearing, everything was going into place. Everything was going so well for the three friends. Betsy thought that they were all going to separate. What a thrill it was going to be to have them all together. But the good Lord was on their sides. Betsy was so overwhelmed with the news and Joey purposing to her, what could get any better then that. She didn't know if she could get any happier then she was at this moment. When it was time to crown the king and queen, it wasn't very hard to guess who it was going to be. Mr. Hale the principal announced the winners. When he called out that Betsy and Joey were the king and queen the spotlight shone right on them. Betsy was so excited, she didn't expect anything like this. Betsy and Joey went up on stage to get crowned. They gave a little speech after they were crowned. They left the stage and went to start the final dance of the night. After the dance was over all of the friends in the school hugged each other and said their good-byes. Most of them didn't knows when or where they would ever meet again.

Betsy went and hugged her teachers and thanked them for everything through the years. She told them that she really enjoyed their classes. And that it was very interesting over the years at sometimes.

The teachers told her that it was a pleasure for them to have her in their class. When she had finally finished saying good-bye Joey took Betsy home.

Betsy couldn't wait to get home and tell her aunt about the wonderful night she had. And to show her the beautiful engagement ring that Joey had given to her. While they were sitting in the limo on the way home Joey told her how much he loved her. Betsy told him that she loved him too and she had wished that her parents were alive to see this and to share in all her precious moments in her life.

Joey told her that they were already there and that they would always be there for her all she had to do was close her eyes and they would be right beside her.

Betsy told Joey that her parents would be so happy and pleased with the decision that she had made tonight when she accepted his purposal.

She knew that they would have loved him just as much as she do. When they reached the ranch Joey and Betsy got out of the limo and thanked the limo driver. Then they went inside. Aunt Elaine knew something was going on because of the smiles that they had hidden across their faces.

Betsy was so happy that she could hardly tell her aunt that Joey had purposed to her. All she could do was show her the engagement ring. Then her aunt knew why they were so happy. Her aunt thought that the ring looked so elegant. Joey bid his good-night to Betsy and he gave her a slow-passionate kiss good-bye. He told her that he would see her in the morning. He also told her that he had a surprise for her. Betsy was so blessed to have found a guy that loved her so much. When Joey left Betsy went upstairs to get undressed and put on something more comfortable. She came back downstairs and she went outside on the porch swing. It was a lovely night and Betsy was telling her aunt all about her night. She told her that it was one of the happiest nights that she has ever had in her life. She just wished her parents were here to share it with her. Aunt Elaine told her that they were there in her heart and in spirit. It was getting late so they went inside and turned in for the night.

When Betsy got upstairs to her bedroom she knelt down and prayed and thanked God for all the blessings in her life. She thanked him for sending her aunt to her and for sending Joey into her life.

While she was praying it was as if her parents were right there beside her. She felt a peaceful feeling come over her.

When she had finished praying she took a shower and went to bed. The next morning when she woke up the sun was shining and she could smell fresh coffee brewing. It was so peaceful just lying there in bed and looking out the window and listening to the birds singing. Betsy didn't even want to get out of bed it was so nice. All of a sudden there was knock on her bedroom door. She sang out and told them to come in but no one did. Betsy thought that it was her aunt at the door but she was wrong. She went to get back into bed but another knock came on the door. This time she decided to open the door. When she opened the door no one was there. She looked around and all she found was a white rose on the floor in the hallway. There was a note attached to it. The note read, "to find true love you have to follow the path of white roses and your true love well be waiting for you at the end of the trail". Betsy knew where the rose came from.

She was a little curious so she got dressed and did what the note said. After all she had nothing to lose but a lot to gain. Betsy walked down the hallway until she found another rose. She walked a little farther and found another rose at her aunts bedroom door. The last rose had another note and it read," if you know me like I think you do then come to me". Betsy knew right where to go.

Betsy took all the roses with her and went to the gazebo in the backyard. And sure enough that was where she found him. Joey had a breakfast prepared for her that was fit for a queen, she was speehless. Joey gave her a good morning kiss and asked her to be seated. Betsy felt so loved at that moment. He had fresh strawberries and they were Betsy's favourite fruit. When Betsy sat down he kissed her neck. She thought that it was so sweet and it tickled a little but she didn't mind. Just the little things that Joey did for her showed her just how much he really loved her. He didn't have to give her any expensive gifts to show her that he cared. She loved being around him and she knew that her parents would have loved being around him as well. Her aunt just adored Joey and everyone that knew him thinks that he is the best kind of person that anyone could get along with. Joey loved doing things for Betsy but he didn't have to prove anything to her because she already knew that he loved her. Just the little were sometimes better then the big things. Having Joey in her life meant everything to her. The breakfast looked and tasted delicious. The morning breeze was so nice and warm. After breakfast Betsy and Joey went for a nice long walk in the fields. They walked until they came to the rivers edge. The river was so calm and blue it was so breathtaking and the view was so exquisite. It was so peaceful at the river it was a great place to think. Betsy rode Blazing Snow by the river many times but she never really stopped to look at it. They sat by the edge of the river and cuddled for awhile and talked about their future. It was getting late and they didn't realize the time. It was getting close to lunchtime. Joey asked Betsy to close her eyes and told her not to peek. While she closed her eyes Joey went and took a picnic basket from behind a tree that he had put there earlier that morning. Joey asked her to please keep her eyes closed for a little longer and she said ok. she asked what he was doing and he told her that she would find out in due time. He sat out a blanket. He had cheese, grapes, soda and fried chicken and a few other things to eat. When he had everything laid out he told her that she could open her eyes.

She was shocked and very surprised when she opened her eyes, she never expected a picnic lunch as well. She asked him when he had done this and Joey told Betsy he would always make time for her. And that he would always plan special moments for her. Moments that she would always remember and treasure. When they had finished eating lunch they packed everything back into the picnic basket. They just sat there for awhile. Joey held her so close to him. Just looking at the river it was so refreshing and peaceful and quiet.

Joey started to sing to her it was so romantic.

While he was singing Betsy fell asleep in his arms.

He didn't want to move her she looked so beautiful.

All the while he was looking at her his eyes were getting tired and he fell asleep as well. Time past and it grew dark. Aunt Elaine was getting worried and wondered where they had gotten off to because it was getting late. She thought something might have happened to them so she got on her horse and she took Blazing Snow with her. She took a flashlight with her and followed the beaten down grass in the fields. When she came to the river she saw Joey and Betsy sound asleep under the big oak tree. They looked so comfortable there together. Aunt Elaine tapped Joey and he was so surprised. When he looked up and saw aunt Elaine standing there her didn't know what to say. Betsy woke with a fright. They didn't realize how late it really was. Joey and Betsy rode Blazing Snow back to the ranch and aunt Elaine rode behind them.

When they reached the ranch house there was a nice fire started in the fireplace for them. It was so pleasant and warm.

Betsy caught a little chill while she was at the river. Aunt Elaine went and made some hot choccolate for everyone. Joey went to get Betsy a sweater to put on. The hot chocolate just hit the spot, it tasted so good and creamy. While they were sitting by the fire it was as if the sparks were dancing. It was so lovely to watch it. The fire seemed like magic and they could have watched it for hours. The fire started to die down so Joey put another couple logs on the fire. Betsy loved the smell of burning wood. Aunt Elaine asked them all about their graduation night. She wanted to hear all about it from Joey. She asked how long he was thinking about asking Betsy to marry him. He told her that he was thinking about it for a long time.

But he wanted to find the right time to ask her and he figured that graduation night would be the right time and he was so right. He made Betsy one of the happiest girls in the world that night. Joey sat down by the fire with Betsy when a knock came on the door. It was Jill, Betsy wondered why she was out at the ranch so late.

The news spread so quickly that Betsy and Joey were missing that she wanted to get to the ranch as soon as possible to see if it was true. Betsy told her that they only fell asleep at the river. Jill thought that it was something more serious. Aunt Elaine gave Jill some hot chocolate and told her that it would calm her nerves. They all started to laugh.

It sounded so funny the way that aunt Elaine said it. It was getting late and Joey had to leave. Joey gave Betsy a good night kiss and told her to take a warm bath and try to get some sleep. She thanked him for the great day. Joey gave Jill a ride home after al she only lived a mile away. Jill was in great shape she didn't mind it because she ran track and field in highschool. When Joey and Jill left the ranch Betsy said good-night to her aunt. She went upstairs and took a shower before going to bed.

When she finished with her shower she went straight to bed because she was so tired.

The summer was almost over and Betsy was doing a lot of thinking about college. She would soon have to leave the ranch. And all of her friends that she made on the ranch. But mostly she was going to miss her aunt Elaine and Blazing Snow.

She was going to miss riding her. Betsy loved that horse so much. She was one of the joys in her life.

The day before Betsy had to leave for college aunt Elaine gave Betsy, Joey and Jill and going away party. They were all going to leave to go to college together so she decided to give them one all together. She invited all of their friends and family members so they all could say good-bye to them at the party. Everyone was having a great time. There were lots of singing and dancing at the party. Betsy, Joey and Jill thanked everyone for coming to the party and wishing them a safe and great trip. The party was starting to die down so the three friends went for a final walk around the ranch.

They couldn't believe that they were leaving in the morning to go to college. They wondered where the years went. They all had so many great times together on the ranch and everywhere else, since they all met eachother. The years went by so quickly. Betsy went to the stable to take Blazing Snow for a ride and Joey and Jill took another horse.

After all it was going to be the last ride that she would take for a very long time. Blazing Snow loved having Betsy stroke her coat. Betsy treated her as though she was a child. Betsy always gave her a sugar cube as a treat. Blazing Snow also loved juicy carrots. The three friends saddled up the horses and rode them into the countryside for one last ride. It was so peaceful and lovely out there in the countryside.

Blazing Snow was really going to miss Betsy just as much as Betsy was going to miss her. It was getting late so the three friends decided it was time to go back to the ranch. When they arrived back to the ranch they saw that all their family and friends were leaving. They were going to miss them all so much. But it was time to move on in their lives.

Having all three of them being accepted to the same college was great, they would always be together. And the best thing about it was that they were all going to be staying in the same dorm. It was a good thing that the dorm had turned co-head when they put the horses back in the stables they went back into the house.

Aunt Elaine was waiting in the house for them.

She had gifts for each of them. But she wanted to give it to them when they were all alone away from everyone. She didn't want anyone to know right yet what she had to tell Betsy and her friends. Aunt Elaine gave Jill he gift first and asked her if she would read the note out loud for all to hear. Jill read "Dear Jill, I wanted to thank-you for being Betsy's best friend. You were so sweet and kind to her when she first came here. And for that I want you to accept this gift and no questions asked. I love you Jill, love aunt Elaine. When Jill opened the gift it was a cheque for five thousand dollars. Jill was speechless. She didn't know what to say, it was unbelievable. Jill gave her a great big hug and a kiss and said thank-you. Then it was Joey's turn.

She gave him a envelope and he read the note first. It read, "Dear Joey, please accept this gift as a token of my gratitude. I wanted you to know that I think of you as the son that I always wanted. I think you are the best thing that ever came into Betsy's life accept for Jill. Her parents would have been so proud to know you as I do. And for that please accept this gift from me." I love you, aunt Elaine. Joey took out the cheque and it was also for five thousand dollars. Joey was so shocked. He told her that she didn't have to give him anything for loving Betsy. He said she was worth far more then any money can buy. But, he knew that she wanted him to have it so he accepted it with great joy. He told her that he would put it to good use and he was going to use it for college and nothing else.

He said thank-you and gave her a big hug and kiss too. It was Betsy's turn and it was going to be a little harder to do. Because she didn't know how Betsy was going to react. So she started out asking Betsy a few questions. The first question was how she would feel if there was another woman in the world that thought of her as a daughter. Betsy already knew how her aunt felt about her. She knew she meant herself and she was fine with that because she loved her just as much. Second question she asked was how would she feel if she found out that she was adopted. This was starting to get a bit confusing to Betsy. She didn't know where her aunt was going with this. Betsy asked her what she was talking about. Aunt Elaine asked her to please hear her out and to please understand what she was about to tell her. She told Betsy that she would understand if she hated her for it. But she thought that it was about time for Betsy to know the truth. And that is why she wanted her to have her friends there with her. Betsy opened the envelope. Inside she found a birth certificate and on it, it said baby girl born to Elaine Simpson.

And also in the envelope there were adoption papers saying that Betsy's parents had adopted her when she was born. Aunt Elaine started to cry and she got up to walk away, but Betsy stopped her and asked her to please sit down and explain all this to her. At this time everyone was speechless.

Joey and Jill just sat there in amazement. But Betsy asked the question, "WHY?"

Aunt Elaine was crying so hard at this point and so was Betsy. She told her she would understand if she didn't want anything else to do with her. Betsy told her not to talk that way. She told her that she was trying to understand everything. And that she would never leave her. She loved her so much to let this get in the way of that love. But Betsy still wanted to know how and why. Aunt Elaine told her that when she was sixteen that she had gotten pregnant by her boyfriend. He was in the army and he had gotten killed while they were practicing. And she couldn't take the pain and the responsibility of a child at such a young age all alone. She knew that her sister couldn't have any children of her own and she wanted a child so much. Her sister had just gotten married and they wanted a baby so badly. So her sister and her new husband adopted Betsy. Aunt Elaine gave her the name that she has.

It was her fathers mothers name her grandmother.

When aunt Elaine finished telling her the story of how it all happened the room stayed so quiet.

Betsy had her head hung down so low she didn't know what to say at that moment. She didn't know if she should look up or not. She was crying so much. To hear that news was such a shock to her.

There was another envelope that she hadn't open yet. It was a letter from her parents. Her mother gave it to her sister just in case anything might happen to them before Betsy went to college. Betsy read it out loud. It said, "Our dearest Betsy, by the time you read this you should be getting ready to go off to college. And you should have been told about being given up for adoption by your real mother. Please don't get mad or hate us or her for keeping this from you. But we wanted to tell you when we knew that you would be capable of taking it like a woman and not a child. We bet you turned out to be a beautiful young woman. Your birth mother my sister and

I love you so much and I hope she knows that we are so grateful to her for blessing us with her child. We know it was hard for her to give you up. She was to young to take care of you all alone and just losing her boyfriend was hard enough on her. So we took you and raised you and loved you as our own. Elaine don't know this but please tell her that I love her so much. You would have loved your father he was a kind and precious man. So please understand why your mother gave you to us. It wasn't because she didn't love you because she did. That's why she did what she had to do. We love you, mom and dad.

Elaine went to walk away she felt has if she needed to get out of that room as quickly as possible. But Betsy got up and grabbed her by the arm.

When Elaine looked back at Betsy she hugged her so tightly. Betsy told her that she understood why she did it. Betsy told her that she loved her so much and that would never change. Betsy could never hate her. Elaine was so relieved. She thought that Betsy would hate her for it. Betsy asked her if she had a picture of her real father.

She wanted to see what he looked like. Elaine went upstairs and brought down a picture of him for her to see. When she came back down from upstairs she handed Betsy a picture of her real father. He was so handsome. He was wearing his army uniform. Betsy sat back down on the couch and just stared at the picture of her father. She couldn't believe how much she looked like him. Betsy asked Jill and Joey to look at the picture of him. Joey said that she looked just like him. And Jill said that he was so handsome and that he looked like a kind soul. Betsy asked if she could keep the picture of him. Aunt Elaine told her that she could and that she had more pictures of him if she wanted them.

Betsy couldn't take her eyes of the picture. Betsy was so drawn to the picture of her real father. Betsy asked her aunt Elaine what he was really like and if he was funny. Elaine told her that he was just like Joey very kind and passionate. And that he was a very loving and understanding. She never met anyone else that could compare to him so that is why never ever married. She never even tried to find anyone else like him because she knew that she would so that is why she lived by herself all this time. Elaine told Betsy that his name was Joseph and that he was in heaven and that he was looking down and watching them as they speak. She could feel hid presence in the room. Betsy always wondered how she got the ranch she thought that it was from a late husband. It seems that when Elaine's father died he gave the ranch to her to take care of.

Betsy's adopted mom didn't want the ranch so then Elaine took it over. Her father wanted to keep the ranch in the family. And he wanted it to keep going on after he had passed. It seemed that Elaine had loved horses as well when she was growing up.

How could she not when she was raised up around them.

Betsy felt something hard in the envelope. And when she looked inside she found a key. She asked what the key was for. Elaine wasn't sure if Betsy wanted the other gift now. But she told her it was a key to a new car for when she went to college.

Elaine knew this and since her parents were killed so suddenly she decided to buy it for her. She asked Betsy if she still wanted it. Betsy accepted the car and gave her a big hug and thanked her for everything else as well. She was so thankful and grateful to her for taking her into her home. Elaine told her that the ranch would always be her home.

She asked Betsy what she could do to pay up for not telling her the truth earlier. Betsy told her not to worry about it and that she was already paid back for all of that. She told her real mother that she never turned her back on her when she needed her the most in her life when her parents were killed in that plane crash. Betsy was so grateful for that. Betsy loved her aunt, "NO" her real mom so much already so this news that she had just told her never harmed her love for her. It was getting late and Joey, Betsy and Jill had to leave the next day for college. Joey said good-night to Elaine and thanked her again for the gift. He gave Betsy a kiss good-night and told her that everything would be just fine. Betsy told him that she knew that everything would be okay. Joey went upstairs to go to bed. Jill also wished Elaine good-night and thanked her again for the gift. Jill told Betsy that she would be up in her room waiting for her. Betsy told her that she would be just fine and not to wait up for her. Elaine said she was going to turn in for the night as well. Betsy asked her if she could stay up with her a little longer so they could talk some more she said it was ok and she thought that they needed to talk alone. Betsy asked her if it was ok if she called her mom instead of aunt Elaine from now on.

Betsy really missed saying mom and she didn't think that her adopted mom would mind if she called her real mom that. Elaine was speechless, she didn't know what to say at first. It came to her as a shock. She said that it was just fine with her if that was really what Betsy wanted. She told her that she needed to say it because she missed it so much. It would really make her whole life feel complete again. And she thought her parents would be fine with it. Elaine said that it would be a great joy to finally hear her daughter call her mom. After all this time it would feel so good. They both knew it was going to be a little awkward for awhile to hear and it would sound funny for awhile but they knew in time they would get used to it, and it was be as if they were saying it all their lives. Betsy told her that she wanted to call her mom for the longest time.

And she didn't know how to ask her if she could.

But now that her real mom told her everything and told her who she really was Betsy knew it wasn't going to be that hard to adjust in calling her mom.

After they had finished talking Betsy and her mom went upstairs for the night. Betsy walked her mom to her bedroom door and gave her a kiss and hug good-night. Her mom had tears in her eyes. Betsy told her that everything was going to be just fine and to get used to being called mom from now on.

Her mom hugged her so tight and wished her a good-night. She told her that she loved her so much and she would see her in the morning. Betsy went to her room and Jill was already asleep, so Betsy wouldn't disturb her. Betsy took a shower before she went to bed. When she had finished she just laid there in bed and stared at her father's picture. She thought that he was so good looking.

She really wished she knew him. But she knew that he was in heaven with her parents watching over her. Jill looked so peaceful while she was sleeping.

Betsy didn't want to bother her to talk so she just let her sleep. Betsy said her prayers as usual like she did every night since her parents were killed.

But this time was a little different for her she had thanked God for giving her real mom back to her.

When she was finished she said "AMEN". She just laid there in bed and thought about the news that she had heard tonight. It was a shock to her. Some thing that she never dreamed off or expected to happen to her. But she was old enough to understand the reasons why her mother gave her up to her sister for adoption. Betsy gave her father's picture a kiss good-night and then she drifted of to sleep.

The next morning the sun was shining and the room was so bright it felt so cheery. Jill woke up first and she was looking at Betsy sleeping. Betsy was holding her father's picture. Jill sneezed and it woke Betsy up. They laughed so hard they thought it was so funny. Betsy asked Jill if she would like to have some fun on their last day at home. Jill agreed that it might be kind of fun. They jumped out of bed and tip-toed across the hallway to Joey's room. Betsy slowly opened the bedroom door. He was sound asleep and he looked so handsome while he was sleeping he was just like a prince. He looked so peaceful but he wasn't going to be peace ful for long. Betsy knelt down at one side of his bed and Jill knelt down on the other side. Betsy started to tickle his nose and when he stirred she ducked down beside his bed. They were both picking at him for awhile. But, when Betsy went to touch him on the face he grabbed her and kissed her and said, "good morning beautiful". She was so surprised it startled her. They thought he was still sleeping. But he was awake for awhile and he was just waiting for the right chance to grab Betsy.

Jill asked if they smelled what she was smelling.

They did and it smelled wonderful. Betsy and Jill went back to their room to get dressed. Joey got dressed as well. They all met in the hallway when they were done. They all went downstairs together.

Joey and Jill both greeted Elaine with a big smile and said good-morning. Betsy went and kissed her on the cheek ans said, "good morning mom". Her mom said, "good morning sweetie". Betsy told Joey that she decided to call Elaine mom from now on.

They thought that is was a great idea. Joey told Betsy that he was so proud of her for taking this like a woman instead of behaving like a child. They sat down to a delicious breakfast. Betsy's mom had out done herself this time with the breakfast. She prepared eggs, bacon, pancakes, toast, fresh squeezed orange juice a fresh brewed coffee. It tasted so delicious. They told her that it was the best breakfast that they had eaten in a long time.

Joey said that the one thing that he was going to miss the most when he goes to college was the home cooking. He said that there was nothing like good old down home cooking. Jill said the things she was going to miss the most were her pets. And Betsy added that she was going to miss Blazing Snow and her new mother the most. Elaine said that the ranch wasn't going to be the same with them all gone. It was going to be very lonely. She has gotten so used to having them all around. She said that she can't wait for the holidays to come so they can all come home for Christmas.

Betsy told he mom that she had a lot to do while they were gone. Her mother wondered what she was talking about. She told her that she and Joey had finally chose their wedding date. It was going to be on Christmas Day, her mother was so happy. Betsy told her mom that she could pick whatever she wanted for the wedding preparerations because they wouldn't have time to plan anything. Her mom was just fine with that and told her that she was going to give them a wedding that they would never forget. But Betsy wanted to decide two things. She asked Jill if she would be her maid of honour and Jill gladly accepted. And Betsy wanted to pick the colours. She wanted burgundy and gold. Her mother told her that she had wonderful taste in her decisions. Betsy's mom insisted that she would pay for everything. The clothes, food, music, etc . . . . Joey and Betsy both said, "thank-you".

It was getting late and it was almost time to leave. It was going to be hard to leave but they knew they had to. Betsy, Joey and Jill loaded up the car. Betsy went to the stable to say good-bye to Blazing Snow. She gave her a kiss on the forehead and told her that she would be back real soon. She was going to miss her horse so much.

When she had finished saying good-bye to her horse she went back to the car. Joey and Jill already said their good-byes to Elaine and waited for Betsy in the car. Betsy started to cry when she reached the car. She hugged her mom and gave her a kiss good-bye. And told her not to worry,they would be just fine. She asked her mom to please take care of Blazing Snow and herself. Her mother told her that she would and hat she loved her very much. Betsy told her mom that she loved her too.

Betsy gave her one last hug and got into the car.

They waved good-bye has they drove off. It was a ten hour drive to the college dorm. They stopped a couple times to use the washrooms and to get snacks. They all took turns driving. Finally they arrived at the dorm. The place was so big and there were so many people there. Parents were there with their kids helping then to move into their dorm rooms. The college was just across the street.

Betsy, Joey and Jill went inside the college to register. Betsy and Jill were so lucky for they were going to be room mates. And Joey was just going to be across the hall from them. When they had finished getting registered they went to the car to get their luggage. The three friends put their luggage in their rooms. When they were finished unpacking they all went shopping for some furniture.

They needed things for their rooms. While they were driving they came across a flea market. They found all the furniture that they needed and bought it all for a great price. A few things they would have to fix up but they didn't mind that. The man at the flea market told them that he would deliver it all for them later that day and they said that it would be just fine. The only thing that they needed were computers. They went to the computer store that was going out of business. They bought their computers and everything that they need to go with the computers for half price. And that was a great bargain. They couldn't believe the hreat deals they were getting. They also went and stocked up on snack foods. They were going to buy their main meals at the cafeteria.

By the time they got back to their dorm rooms all their furniture was delivered there. It took them a little while to unpack everything and put everything in the right places. By the time they were done it was almost time to go to bed. They were all so tired and Betsy gave Joey a kiss good night and then he went to his room to go to bed. Before Betsy went to bed she gave her mother a phone call to let her know that they were all settled into their rooms.

She told her that Jill was her room mate and Joey was just across the hall from her. Her mom thought that it was great that they were all together.

Her mom was so glad to hear her voice. Betsy was getting sleepy so she told her mom that she loved abd wished her good-night. Her mom told her to it easy and to say hi to Jill and Joey for her. She told Betsy that she could call her anytime of the day or night. Her mom told her that she loved and said good-night. Betsy hung up the phone and said her prayers like she did every night. When she had finished she went straight to bed and before long she was sound to sleep.

The next morning Jill and Betsy woke up about the same time. They took turns taking a shower.

They got dressed and met Joey in his room. They all went to the college cafeteria to get some breakfast. They ordered a good breakfast but it didn't taste half as good as home cooking. By the time they were finished breakfast it was time to get ready to go to their first class. They all had different classes because they were not going for the same goal in life. Betsy went to business head and Joey went to a class to help him study to become a veterinarian. And Jill went to class that would help her study to become a doctor. They were all so lucky to have found the same college that taught all those subjects. It felt a little awkward going to different classrooms at first and not having their friends in the same class room with them. But they would get used to it and after all they would see each other during breaks. They met all kinds of new people during class and they came from all parts of the world. It didn't take long for them to get used to be alone in the class room without each other. School work was piling up and soon they never had much time for anything. But they always found time to spend with each other, especially Betsy and Joey. When all the rest were out partying the three friends would stay in and study.

They wanted to get good grades. And they sure did at that. They were at the tops of their classes. Most of the other people thought that the three friends were a little stuck up but they didn't care what the other people thought of them. They only had one purpose for going to college and that was to be the best they could be in their lives and they were determined to do that. Even if it killed them trying.

But all the hard work paid off because they were doing great in their studies.

It was getting close to Christmas and Joey, Betsy and Jill were getting ready to go back home for the big day. They couldn't wait to get home and to see their families. Betsy could hardly wait to see her mom and Blazing Snow. They were going to be home a week before their wedding day and they wanted to get home before the dirty weather came on. It came over the radio that there was going to be a storm and they wanted to get ahead of the storm. Betsy's mom was terrified that they were going to get caught in the storm. So Betsy and the others left early before the storm came on. When they were half way home the storm started to get harder and harder. Betsy asked Joey if he would take over the driving. She was a little nervous driving in dirty weather. She had never driven in lots of snow before so she didn't know what to expect. Joey didn't mind taking over for Betsy he would do anything for her. The snow was coming on hard and it was piling up on the roads. The snow plow wasn't on the roads yet and it was getting a little difficult to drive in the snow. Joey took his time driving. It wasn't his first time driving in the snow so it didn't bother him that much. Betsy had her cell phone with her so she called her mother and told her that they were on their way and not to worry. She told her that Joey was driving and he was being very careful. Her mother was relieved to hear that. Betsy and friends were so anxious to get home. Jill's and Joey's parents were at te ranch waiting to see them. Betsy's mom told them that they were on their way home. Betsy couldn't wait to see her horse for she sure missed her. The only one that Blazing Snow would let ride her so she could get some exercise was Betsy's mom. The snow was starting to let up a little bit just enough so Joey could see in from of him clearer. It wasn't long when they saw the ranch gate in front of them.

They were so relieved to finally be home. When they reached the house Joey honked the horn and Betsy's mom and the other families came running outside. They didn't mind the snow falling because they didn't even put a coat on. Just having their kids home was enough for them. They were all so happy to see each other again. Betsy ran to her mother she was so happy to see her again. When everyone was finished kissing and hugging they all went inside. Betsy's mom had a great dinner prepared for all of them. Before Betsy could sit down to have dinner she had to go out to the stables to see Blazing Snow. Joey went with her and when they got out to the stable Betsy called out to Blazing Snow. Her horse was so happy to see her.

Betsy ran to her horse and gave her a great big hug she was so happy to have her arms around her horse again. Betsy told Blazing Snow that she would see her again after dinner.

Betsy and Joey went back inside the house to have dinner with their families. The dinner that her mom had prepared tasted so good it was so good to have a home cooked meal. They missed that so much. Home cooking tasted a whole lot better then the cafeteria food. When they all finished dinner they all went into the living room to talk about college and the wedding. Betsy's mom had everything prepared for their wedding day. Joey's parents helped with the wedding also. Betsy's mom didn't want to leave them out of it all. She wanted to get their opinions on some of the preparations as well. They just hoped that Betsy and Joey liked what they had chosen for them. Betsy's mom showed them what they had planned for them.

Betsy loved the colour and make of the dresses that her mom had picked out for the brides girls.

It was just the thing that she would have chosen.

Joey also loved the tuxedos that his mom had picked out for him and his grooms men to wear.

It was only two days away from the wedding and they were all so excited, they could hardly wait.

Betsy's mom had the caterer and music all picked out as well. She had hired a band for the great event. Betsy and Joey could hardly believe that their big day was soon going to be here. She only wished that her parents were alive to see it. But she knew that they would be there in spirit and they would watch over them on their special day. Betsy and Joey were looking over the music when a knock came on the door. Elaine went to answer it.

She opened the door and there was a man there and he said that he had a parcel to deliver to Betsy.

And he told her that only Betsy could open it. The man asked if Betsy was at home and Elaine said yes. Betsy came to the door and when she opened the door again Mrs. Lee was standing in the door way. Betsy was so happy to see her. The taxi driver brought Mrs. Lee's suitcase to the door.

Betsy asked her to come inside out of the cold.

When they got back inside Betsy took her coat and asked her to please come into the living room to meet her fiancee and the rest of the family. Joey gave Mrs. Lee a big hug and told her that he was finally glad to meet her. Mrs. Lee thanked him and told him that she was glad to finally meet him as well. She said that Betsy had told her all about him in her letters. Betsy always wrote to Mrs. Lee and told her about everything that was happening in her life. She also told her that her aunt was really her real mother. And that she was adopted. Mrs. Lee knew that she was adopted and that Elaine was her real mother. But, she couldn't tell Betsy because she promised her parents that she would keep it a secret for them until Betsy was old enough to understand it all. Mrs. Lee was so proud of Betsy and she couldn't believe how beautiful she turned out. She was such a lovely young woman. Mrs. Lee told Betsy that she was right about Joey and that he was a real hottie. Joey started to blush, he didn't know what to say when Mrs. Lee said that. Joey thought that it was so funny. Betsy told him that it was the truth and that she always told the truth.

Betsy told him to get used to it because she was going to call him that for a very long time. Joey told her that he live with that. He loved her so much and everyone could see that. Betsy loved him more then words could say. You could see it in her eyes just how much she loved him. They were perfect for each other.

The day of Betsy's and Joey's wedding finally arrived. Joey and his grooms men went downstairs in the extra family room to get dressed for the wedding. He didn't want to see her until it was time.

Betsy and her brides girls stayed upstairs to get dressed. Betsy's mom had the ranch decorated beautifully. For that was where they were getting married. They didn't want a church wedding. It was a beautiful day for a wedding. The sun was shining and there wasn't a cloud in the sky. Betsy was so nervous that she could hardly believe that the day she dreamed of was finally here. She waited a long time for this day. She knew that Joey was the one for her and that he was going to make her the happiest woman in the world.

The time was drawing near for Betsy and Joey's special moment. All of the guest were gathering in the building that her mom had built for her special day. They just hoped that it didn't snow. But, Betsy didn't really care if it snowed or not nothing was going to spoil her day. Although it was Christmas Day everyone waited to open their presents. This day was for Betsy and Joey. Joey and his grooms men went outside to the building where the wedding was about to start. Everyone that was invited to the wedding were all seated and they were just waiting for Betsy to walk down the aisle. Blazing Snow was attached to a coach to bring Betsy to the building from the ranch. Blazing Snow was draped in flowers. Betsy loved the dress that her mother had picked out for her it was just beautiful.

Betsy's mom was waiting downstairs for her. Her mother started to cry, she was so happy for Betsy.

She couldn't believe that today she would be giving her daughter away for the second time. But this time it will be a happy time. Betsy's dress fitted her perfectly. It was satin with a lot of sequence and diamonds flowing all over it. Her mom told her that she looked absolutely beautiful and that she was so proud of her. She gave her a wrap to put over her dress so she wouldn't get cold while sitting in the coach. They all went outside and got in the coach and headed for the building. Betsy's mom even had a red carpet laid out for her. Her mom wanted this day to be the happiest day of her little girls life and she didn't care what she had to do to make that happen.

When they arrived at the building the doors opened for her to enter. The music started to play and Betsy slowly walked down the aisle on her mothers arm behind her brides girls. When Joey caught a glimpse of her he started to cry. He couldn't believe how beautiful she was. He always knew she was beautiful but today he couldn't keep his eyes of her. Everyone thought that she looked so lovely. Betsy smiled as she walked towards Joey. She was a little better now because she knew that she was about to do the right thing and that she knew that Joey was the only man for her.

While they were saying their vows Betsy started to cry she couldn't keep it in any longer. She didn't want to cry but they were happy tears. Joey started to wipe the tears from her face. He stroke her face so passionately and she felt so warm from his touch. After they had said their vows they lit the candles. Betsy lit a candle for her parents and she read a little poem in memory of them. She just wished that they were there to share in this happy moment in her life but she knew that they were looking down on them and giving then their blessings. They would have been so happy to know Joey for he was a greatest guy that Betsy could have met. He treated her like a queen. After the vows were said and the candles were lit and everything else was said and done the priest pronounced them husband and wife. The priest told Joey that he could kiss his bride. Everyone clapped for them as they walked down the aisle. It was over they finally did it.

The reception was being held in the ranch house. Betsy's mom had enough food prepared for everyone. There was plenty to go around. Everything was going just great. Betsy and Joey cut their wedding cake and they fed each other. When it was time to throw the bouquet all the single ladies gathered around to try and catch it. When Betsy threw it Jill caught it. Betsy told her that it was her turn next. Jill just blushed and said that she would never get married but that was what Betsy said too and look at her now. Jill's turn would come and she would find the right man for her someday. When Joey threw the garter a strange man caught it. He smiled at Jill and she blushed and shied away.

Betsy caught the look that Jill and the strange guy gave each other. Betsy and Joey went around to all the guests and thanked them all for coming and for the lovely gifts. They had a wonderful turn out for their special day.

Joey and Betsy had a lot of money given to them and most of the money would come in handy for when they get back to the college. Betsy and Joey didn't want to go antwhere for their honeymoon they wanted to stay on the ranch with Betsy's mom.

Betsy asked her mom if that was ok with her and her mom told her that the ranch was their home as well. Betsy wanted to spend some time with her horse as well. She really missed her so much and she knew that Blazing Snow missed her just as much. When the reception was starting to die down Betsy and Joey went upstairs to get on a change of clothes. The guest were starting to leave. All the wedding party went to get undressed as well. Betsy and Joey thanked them for helping them make this day a happy one for them. And they were glad to be able to call them friends. The wedding party wished them both a happy life together. They all knew that Betsy and Joey would be happy together Joey had his suitcases in Betsy's room. When they reached the bedroom door Joey told Betsy that she could go in and get undressed first. But Betsy told him that it was just fine with her and that he could go into the room with her after all he was her husband now and they had to get used to seeing each other sooner or later. Joey said he would go in only if she was comfortable with it. She said it was just fine and she wanted him to go into the room with her. When Betsy opened the door she got a big surprise inside. Her bed was covered with white rose pedals and there was a bigger selection of roses all over the room. Betsy started to cry and she turned to Joey and thanked him for the wondederful surprise. She told him that he didn't have to do that for her. His love was all she wanted. He told her that he would do anything for his beautiful wife.

Betsy kissed him and told him that she was so happy to be his wife. Joey touched her face ever so gently. He stroked his hands through her beautiful blonde hair. Betsy slowly unbuttoned Joey's shirt.

Joey asked her if it was ok to make love to her. He didn't want to rush her. He knew it was her first time as well as his first time. He wanted to make her feel comfortable. Betsy wanted Joey to make love to her for the longest time now. She told him it was just fine with her if they made love right then and now. She told him that she felt very safe with him and that she knew that he would be very gentle and loving, slowly their clothes started coming off. Joey picked her up in his arms and while he was walking towards the bed he was kissing her passionately.

Betsy loved having her hair stroked. Joey slowly caressed Betsy's body. He was so loving and gentle. Betsy couldn't believe how lucky she was.

She was making love to a man that you could only dream about. Butt all of her dreams were coming true. After they had finished making love Joey and Betsy just laid there in bed staring at each other telling each other how much they loved one another. Joey asked Betsy if she would like a glass of wine and she said yes. She don't usually drink but this was a very special occasion. One glass of wine would never hurt her. Joey got out of bed and poured two glasses of wine and also brought a bowl of fresh strawberries and cream back to bed with him.

Betsy just loved strawberries. Betsy and Joey fed each other with the berries and cream. Betsy had some cream on her cheek. She went to wipe it off but Joey asked if he could wipe it off. She told him to go right ahead. She thought he was going to wipe the cream of with a tissue but she was wrong.

Joey leaned over and slowly licked the cream of her cheek with his tongue. His tongue tickled a little ans it felt so warm. That was the first time anyone ever licked her face and Betsy seemed to enjoy it. It seemed unusual to Betsy because all of this was new to her. But she didn't mind it one little bit. Joey asked Betsy if he was hurting her.

That was one thing that he didn't want to do. She asked him to continue. She knew in her heart that he would never hurt her. Everything felt so right.

Joey gave her another passionate kiss and held her in his arms so tightly. Betsy felt so secure laying in her husbands arms. It was getting late and they both drifted back to sleep. It wasn't long when they woke again. It was beautiful outside and the snow had stopped falling. Yesterday was Christmas Day and also their wedding day so they kept today to celebrate the holiday. Joey just laid there looking at Betsy. She was so beautiful and Joey couldn't keep his eyes of her. Joey went to kiss her on her luscious lips and when he did she pulled him back down towards her and told him how much she loved him. Joey told her that she was the sunshine in his hair, the whisper in the wind and that he would always be here for her. They smelled a wonderful aroma coming from downstairs and they knew what it was. It was the lovely scent of her mom's wonderful breakfast. They got out of bed and put on their robes. They were so hungry that they could hardly wait. Joey took Betsy by the hand and they both went downstairs to eat breakfast.

When they got downstairs they both kissed her mom on the cheeks at the same time. They wished a good morning and a merry Christmas. Her mom thanked them and wished them the same thing.

She told them that breakfast was waiting for them on the table in the dining room. Betsy asked why they were eating in the dining room. They usually ate in the kitchen, her mom told her that they would find out when they got in the dining room. Joey brought in the tray of coffee for his new mother-in law. Joey asked Elaine if he could have a word with her in the kitchen. So Betsy went to the dining room and waited for the. Elaine said it was ok to speak alone. She asked him what he wanted and he came right out and asked if it was ok with her if he called her mom instead of Elaine. He said that he would feel more comfortable if he could. Elaine just looked at him and never cracked a smile. Joey thought she might have gotten mad. He told her it was ok if she didn't want him to call her mom. She grabbed him and hugged him so tight. She burst out laughing and told him that she wouldn't have it any other way. Joey was so relieved to hear that.

Elaine put her arm around him and they walked to the dining room to have a wonderful breakfast.

When they sat to the breakfast table there were a few extra people sitting there. Joey and Betsy didn't expect anyone would be joining them for breakfast. Jill and her parents were there, Joey's parents were there as well. Joey hugged his parents first and went to sit by his new wife. He told them that he was so happy to have them there to help share with them for their first Christmas together as man and wife. Betsy was so happy to spend first Christmas with her real mom. Although she spent many Christmas's with her real mom before but this time was different.

Elaine asked Joey if he would say the blessing before they ate the lovely breakfast. He said that he would love to. Joey thanked God first of all for his beautiful wife, then he thanked him for his family and friends and for the delicious meal that they were about to eat. When he had finished saying the blessing they all started to enjoy the delightful meal Joey said that if they didn't cme back home to get married it was worth the long drive just to get home to have some home cooking.

When they had finished eating breakfast they all went in the living room to open their Christmas presents. There were tons of presents under the tree for everyone. They all enjoyed opening their gifts. They didn't care about the mess that they were making with the gift wrap. They were all having such a wonderful time. The mess didn't matter to anyone. Betsy's mom had a gift for them that she hoped that they would accept. It was a little box wrapped in gold paper with a tag that said, "to Joey and Betsy Merry Christmas love mom". Before they opened it Elaine asked them if they could guess what could be in such a small box. They didn't have any idea what could be in such a small box. Joey let Betsy open it. When she opened it she pulled out a key. They were surprised and confused. They didn't know what the key meant or what it was for.

Her mom told them that there was a little note inside as well and she asked Joey if he would read it out loud. Joey unfolded the note it read, "my dearest Betsy and Joey, this is the key that opens the lock to your new house. Although the house is not built yet it well open the lock to your front door.

Only if you accept this key from me. You can have it built wherever you choose. I love you both, Merry Christmas", love mom.

Betsy and Joey didn't know what to say. They were speechless and Betsy asked her mom why she wanted to build them a new house. They told her that she didn't have to build them a new house.

But her mother wanted to and also her parents had a trust fund for her and they wanted to help Betsy's biological mom to help build a dream home for Betsy and her new husband for a wedding present. And since Betsy's adopted parents weren't around to share in Betsy's new life her mom wanted to honour their wishes.

Betsy and Joey said that they would love to accept the wonderful gift but, they had one condition. Her mom wondered what that condition was going to be. Joey told her to stop worrying. The condition was that they would gladly accept the new house if it could be built on the ranch. Her mom was so relieved. She thought it was going to be something else. Her mom told them that she would love to have build their new home on the ranch. She told them that as soon as the snow goes away they would start looking for a terrific contractor to get started on their house. Betsy wanted a patio and french doors in her bedroom overlooking the beautiful luscious green hills. That view was so amazing to look at in the morning.

Especially when there was fresh morning dew on the ground. And how lovely it looked when it rained.

By the time all the presents were opened and all the mess was cleaned up it was getting close to turkey time. Christmas dinner to Joey was more fun to eat then opening presents. He just loved home cooked turkey with all the fixings. Elaine thought of everything. She had turkey, mashed potatoes, and almost everything else you could imagine. Everyone was enjoying dinner. Although it was one day later to celebrate Christmas and a little late to be enjoying such a great dinner it didn't matter to any of them. Just being together was all that mattered to them.

It was getting close for Betsy and Joey to return to college. It was going to be a little different when they get back to the college. They were going to get an apartment close to the dorm and college.

When it was time for Betsy, Joey and Jill to leave all their families met at the ranch to say good-bye.

Betsy and Joey went to the stable to say good-bye to Blazing Snow. Betsy hated having to leave her again but she knew she was going to be ok with her mom. Betsy's mom took real good care of her horse. Betsy gave Blazing Snow a hug and kiss on the forehead. She told her that she would be back real soon and when she comes home this time it will be coming home to stay.

Betsy and her new husband went back to the car to say good-bye. As usual there were tears but they were happy tears. They weren't saying goodbye forever. They all got in the car and drove off. It was a beautiful day for driving in the winter snow.

Betsy still didn't like driving in the winter time so Joey drove all the way back to college. It felt like forever getting there but they finally arrived. All of their friends were returning back from the holidays as well. It was great to see them all again. Betsy,

Joey and Jill started to carry their luggage back into the dorm rooms. Jill moved across the hall in the dorm room Joey had so he could move in with Betsy. The dorm didn't mind them sharing a room because they were married. They only stayed there a few days when they found their own apartment.

They packed up all their things and moved into their new place. They were moving into a two bedroom apartment. What Jill didn't know was that they wanted her to move in with them as well. Joey didn't want Betsy to be alone while he was out doing other things. Jill told them that they needed their privacy and after all they had just gotten married. She thought they wanted to be alone. And on the other hand Jill couldn't afford to pay the rent for a new apartment. Betsy insisted that she move in with them. They weren't going to take any rent money from her.

All they wanted was for her to pay for some of the food bill. Jill didn't know what to say she was so overwhelmed. She asked if it was sure if that was what they really wanted. They told her that they were sure. Jill was so excited she accepted without any thought.

They all packed up their things and carried them down to the moving van. Their new apartment was fully furnished so they whatever they didn't want to their friends. The new apartment was an half hour drive from the college. So that wasn't too bad.

When everything was loaded into the moving van they said good-bye to their friends and told them they were welcomed to come for a visit whenever they wanted. When the van headed out, Betsy,

Joey and Jill followed them in car. The ride didn't seem that long from the campus. The apartment was located in a nice and clean town. When they reached the apartment Joey helped the movers on load the van. Betsy took Jill upstairs to see their new home. Jill thought the place was beautiful. It was bigger then she expected.

Jill said that it was going to be great living with her two best friends. But it still seemed like she was imposing on them. Since they were newly weds and all. But Betsy wouldn't hear of any nonsense they wanted her to stay with them. So the subject was closed. When the men had finished bringing up the furniture and the rest of their belongings Joey gave them a tip and thanked them for their help. It seemed as though there was a lot more stuff. When all the furniture was ion place they all decided to go out for dinner. They all decided to go to a Chinese restaurant. The surroundings were remarkable and the seating area was beautiful. The food was delicious. When the waitress brought the check to the table she also gave them three fortune cookies. Betsy just loved reading fortune cookies.

She asked if she could read hers first. They said it was just fine with them. Betsy broke open the cookie and read, "long life, romance and the love of her life is near". Joey opened his cookie and it read, "beauty surrounds you and good fortune ahead". They both knew that their cookies were right. It was Jill's turn, she broke open the cookie and it read, "your turn will come, love and riches awaits you". She started to laugh and said she hopes she wins the lottery soon. They all started to laugh it was so funny. Joey went and paid for the dinner. When they left the restaurant Jill met up with a old friend of hers. Her friend's name was Brady. He asked her if she would like to go for a cup of coffee with him. She introduced Brady to Betsy and Joey. They said that it was a pleasure to meet him. Brady said that it was a pleasure also.

Jill told them that she would see them back at home in a few hours. They bid their good-night and drove off. Betsy and Joey drove back to the apartment. When they reached home they decided that they would leave everything for the morning to unpack. They were so tired so they just went to bed for the night. It was awhile before Jill came home.

Betsy heard her open the apartment door Joey was sound asleep. Jill tiptoed to her bedroom so she wouldn't wake Betsy and Joey. But she didn't know that Betsy was awake. When she heard Jill's bedroom door close she slowly drifted of to sleep.

The next morning Jill was the first one out of bed. She was full of energy. She unpacked a lot of their things while Betsy and Joey were sleeping.

Jill made breakfast for everyone. Joey and Betsy awoke almost about the same time. They could smell fresh coffee brewing and it smelled really good. They got out of bed and went out into the kitchen. Jill had the table filled with toast, eggs, bacon and pancakes. Joey told her that she didn't have to cook all of that but she said that she wanted to make herself useful after all she was staying there for rent free. Betsy and Joey loved Jill so much. They couldn't imagine life without her in it.

Jill's breakfast was delicious. Joey told the girls to go do what they had to do while he did the dishes.

So they went and got ready for class. When they had finished getting ready and Joey got dressed they all left for class. It seemed a little funny for Betsy and Joey to return to college as husband and wife. But they didn't mind it they loved the sound of it. It seemed a little funnt for Betsy to call herself Mrs. Malone. But she knew it wasn't going to be long before she got used to it. When Jill arrived at class she bumped into a guy that she thought she had met before. She told him she was sorry. He said he wasn't and said it was just fine. He told her he didn't mind getting bumped into a pretty girl first thing in the morning, Jill blushed. She knew that she had seen him somewhere before. Finally it came to her. It was the guy that caught the garter at Betsy's wedding. He introduced himself to Jill his name was Isaac. She told him her name and told him she was so pleased to meet him. Isaac just arrived at the college. He was new there and he came all the way from New York City. Isaac told Jill that he was so glad that she bumped into him. It was great to see a friendly face. Jill and Isaac seemed to hit it of perfectly.

Weeks passed by quickly and it seemed that Jill and Isaac were spending a lot more time with each other. It seemed to Betsy and Joey that the relationship between them was blooming just like a vibrant rose. Betsy that Isaac was the man for Jill.

And they knew it also. Isaac took Jill out for dinner and asked her if she would like to move in with him.

Jill was so surprised she never expected it. Jill told him that she would think about it. When Jill got home from the date she asked Betsy what she thought about the idea of her moving in with Isaac.

Betsy told her that if she felt in her heart that it was the right thing to do and if she truly loved Isaac then she would know if she was doing the right thing. Jill told Betsy that she truly loved him and he told her the same thing. She told Betsy that was knew what she was going to do and she was going to give it a try. The next day Jill told Isaac that she would love to move him with him and that made him so happy. Isaac and Jill went to her apartment and packed up all her things to move into her new place with the love of her life. When everything was packed up Joey told Jill and Isaac that they were welcomed back there at any time. Jill gave them both a kiss and hug good-bye and told them not to worry. Everything was going to be just fine. Isaac promised Betsy that he would take real good care of Jill. Betsy knew that she would be just fine. Isaac was a terrific guy and she knew that he was the perfect guy for Jill, they had so much in common.

When Jill and Isaac left Betsy started to cry.

Joey told her that everything was going to be just fine. He knew that Isaac really loved Jill. Joey told her that he could see the lover in Isaac's eyes whenever he looked at Jill. Betsy knew that Joey was right because that's what she see when she looks in his eyes. Betsy was very happy that Jill found someone to share her life with. It was getting late so they went to bed. It was going to be a long day tomorrow. They were going to take their finals and they studied long and hard. They wanted to graduate so they could go back home to start up their own businesses.

Betsy's mom called and told them that their house was finished. Her mother told her that she hoped that Joey didn't mind but she added an extra piece into the house. She added a veterinarians clinic to the house and it was fully loaded with everything he needed, so he wouldn't have to worry about anything. Betsy told Joey and he was speechless. He was so overwhelmed he didn't know what to say.

He told Betsy what if he didn't pass all his courses.

Betsy's mom said that she knew that he was going to pass and that's why she did it. Joey told Elaine that he loved her so much and that he wanted to thank her from the bottom of his heart. She said she would do anything for her son. Joey started to cry and passed Betsy the phone. She asked him what was wrong. He told her that her mother called him son and that touched him so much. Betsy told her mom that they loved her so much and they wanted to thank her for everything. Then Betsy said good-bye to her mom and hung up the phone. A few weeks had pasted and Betsy and Joey received their grades in the mail. They were so nervous they weren't sure if they wanted to open them. So Betsy opened Joey's and he opened hers. They both looked very sternly at the papers and just about the same time they both screamed out loud.

When they both screamed they gave each other their own papers. They were so thrilled with their grades. They both passed with honours. They were at the top of their class. What an achievement for both of them. Betsy called her mom and told her the good news her mom was so pleased. She told her that she knew in her heart that they would do well. She also told them that as long as they were together great things would happen to them in their lives.

Graduation day was at hand and Betsy and Joey invited Isaac and Jill to go shopping with them for proper attire for their big day. Jill and Isaac accepted so they met them at the mall. When they all arrived at the mall Jill told Betsy that today was the day that she and Isaac were going to look for an engagement ring. Betsy was so happy for her.

Before they went shopping they all went to get something to eat. They were talking about the good times they all had together and how they all met each other. They were all so happy that they found one another. When all the reminiscing was through and they had finished lunch they split up and went shopping. Betsy and Jill went into a boutique that had radiant gowns. They didn't know which one to choose they were all so beautiful. Jill found the gown that she wanted it was silver covered in fine lace. Betsy picked out one that was gold. The gown was pure satin with diamonds around the neckline ans waistline. Their gowns were just radiant. They couldn't wait to wear them to their graduation. It took them a long time to get to this day and they deserved it. The two friends only knew each other for fifteen years so it was long enough for them to become more like sisters then just friends. They would never break that bond. It was a bond that would live with them forever. When they paid for the gowns they went looking for Joey and Isaac.

At the same time the men were looking for them.

When they all met up with each other Isaac asked Jill if she wanted to go and look at the engagement rings next. Jill agreed it was time for them to go and browse the jewellery stores. They both said goodbye to Betsy and Joey. Betsy told them that they would see them later. So they all went their seperate ways. Joey and Betsy decided to call it a day and they went home. Betsy was getting a little tired of running around all day. She loved to shop but on this day she seemed to be very tired more then usual. Joey asked her if she was feeling ok. She told him that she just wanted to go home and rest for awhile, so he headed for home. On the way she told Joey that she had a real bad stomach and it hurt really bad. It felt like her something inside her was trying to cut her in half. That's all Joey needed to hear, instead of going home he drove straight to the hospital. It didn't take him long to get there.

When he arrived he took her up in his arms and carried her into the emergency room and asked for help. The nurse put Betsy in a wheelchair and carried her into the examining room. Joey was so afraid he didn't know what was wrong with Betsy.

He called her mother and told her what had happened and that he was waiting to hear from the doctor to see what had happen to her. Her mother said that she was on her way. When Joey had hung up with Elaine the doctor came out of the room to talk to him. He asked Joey to sit down.

Joey didn't know what to expect. Everything was running through his mind. He just hoped it wasn't to serious. The doctor told him that Betsy had a miscarriage. Joey was so shocked he didn't even expect anything like that. He asked the doctor if he could see his wife. The doctor told him that it was just fine but, he had a few more things to explain to them when they get to Betsy's room. The doctor wanted it to be a private conversation and he didn't want anyone else to hear what he had to say. When Joey got to her room she was crying.

She asked Joey to call Jill and he told her that he would. The doctor told him to call her now because he didn't want any disturbances when he told them the news. Joey went to call Jill and when Joey told her what had happen she was speechless. Jill told him that she and Isaac were on there way.

Joey went back to the room and sat beside Betsy on the bed. The doctor told them that the miscarriage that Betsy had was a very serious one. It was so severe that it was going to make it very difficult for her to conceive anymore children. Joey asked the doctor if he was sure if she couldn't get pregnant again. The doctor told him that he was sure.

He told them that Betsy needed some rest and if there was anything that he could then just ask.

When the doctor left the room Betsy cried like a baby. He held her so lovingly. She told him that she was so sorry that she wouldn't be able to give him any children. Joey told her that didn't matter right now just as long has he had her and that she was going to be ok. he told her that they could always adopt but there was no hurry because they had plenty of time to talk about it. It took Betsy's mom a few hours to get to the hospital but she finally arrived. She ran right to Betsy's room. She went and hugged both of them so tightly and told them she was sorry. Joey told her that Betsy wasn't going to be able to have any children of her own.

Her mother told her that everything was going to be just fine and there was a purpose and reason for everything that happens in life, just look what happen to her father. He was taken away before she was born and he would never get the chance to hold his little girl. But she knew that he was with her through it all and that was the main thing.

Knowing that life must go on and just be thankful that they had each other. Betsy knew that her mom was right and that she was so glad that she was there with her in her time of need.

Jill and Isaac came into the room and everything was so quiet. Jill asked what had happened and Joey told her the whole story. Jill felt so sad for her friends and told them that she would do anything they wanted if they needed something. Joey told her that there was nothing she could do right now and not to worry because everythng was going to be just fine.

The next day Betsy was released from the hospital. Joey and her mother came to pick her up and carried her home. Betsy felt so empty inside even though she didn't know that she had been pregnant. But she knew she would be just fine.

When they arrived home Joey had a bed made up for her on the sofa. He pampered her and told her to rest and not to worry about anything he was going to take care of everything. Her mother made dinner that night. It tasted just like being back home on the ranch. A good home cooked meal hit the spot. Betsy couldn't wait to get back home to see her horse Blazing Snow.

A few days had passed and the graduation was finally here. Joey asked Betsy if she felt up to it to go to her graduation. She said that she would be just fine and that she didn't want to miss it. No one else knew that she lost her baby so it would be ok.

Then there wouldn't be any questions about anything. Betsy and Joey got dressed and met Jill and Isaac at the college. The reception area was crowded. All of the graduates looked really sheik in their outfits. Betsy's mom found her seat and waited for the graduating ceremony to begin. It seemed like it was taking forever but that was just because there were so many graduates that had to get ready. Finally the time came for it to start. Betsy's mom as well has all the rest of the parents were so proud of their children. Elaine was so happy that she found her daughter after all these years and that Betsy accepted that she was her mother.

Elaine started to cry when she saw Betsy and Joey walking up the aisle. Jill and Isaac were behind them. Betsy was so happy she had everything she wanted. A terrific mother, a loving husband, her best friend and of course her horse. She was very grateful for the life that was given to her. When all the graduates received their diplomas everyone cheered and clapped. And the tradition continued, when the drums started to beat, up went the graduating hats. There was hats flying everywhere. All you could see was a shower of blue hats, it looked so pretty. During the reception all of the graduates signed each others year books. They were all wishing each other the best in their lives ahead. When the reception was over Betsy and Joey decided to leave. Betsy was getting really tired. She wished everyone well and said good-night. Betsy said good night to Jill and Isaac and told them that she would see them tomorrow before they leave to go back home on the ranch. Betsy and Jill hugged each other and said good-night.

Joey carried Betsy and her mom back to the apartment. They couldn't believe it was finally over.

All of the years and hard work they had put into college had finally paid off. Betsy could finally go home and be with Blazing Snow and not have to leave her anymore. And to do something with her life that she really loved and enjoyed. When they arrived at the apartment Betsy's mom went straight to bed. Betsy and Joey decided to go to bed as well it was getting late and they had a long day ahead of them. They turned out the lights and went to bed it was early when they awoke the next morning. As usual Elaine was making breakfast. It smelled divine and tasted great. They had a lot of packing to do before the moving van arrived. When they had finished breakfast they started to pack everything into boxes. Betsy couldn't wait to get back home on the ranch. Jill and Isaac arrived just in time. They were all packed up when the moving van arrived. Isaac helped Joey carry things out to the van. Jill and Betsy sat and talked awhile. They both hated to say good-bye but they knew that they had to it sooner or later. They talked about their highschool years and how they met. They would never forget each other. They were more like sisters and they promised that they would keep in touch and visit one another from time to time. After all the tears were wiped away it was time to leave.

Jill told Joey to take of himself and to take care of her best friend for her. He promised her that he would. Betsy, Joey and her mother got into the car and drove away. Betsy hated to have to leave Jill but she knew that she would be ok and that they would be talking to each other real soon. Betsy also knew that she had her life to live with her new husband and her new career. It wasn't long before they finally reached the ranch. Betsy couldn't believe the house that her mother had built for them. It was as big as the ranch house and just as beautiful. Joey's clinic was also joined onto the house. They would be working together as well as living together.

While the movers were unpacking the van Betsy and Joey went to see Blazing Snow. Betsy was so happy to see her horse again. She hadn't seen her in such a long time. Blazing Snow was so excited to see Betsy, she started to cry when she hugged her horse. Her horse was getting old and she wasn't as active as she once was but she still had some pluck in her yet. It felt so good to put her fingers through her beautiful white mane. Blazing Snow was just as beautiful as ever. Joey knew that Betsy was longing to see her horse again. It was as if it was her child. To Betsy blazing Snow seemed to be a child. She had her for such a long time. It was getting late so Betsy and Joey went back to their house. They all had dinner and after dinner they unpacked a few things just to keep them going until morning. They were getting tired so they decided to go to bed. Betsy and Joey thanked her mom for everything and bid her good-night. Betsy couldn't get over how beautiful her new house was.

It was a huge dream come true for her. It was like she was in a fairy tale. Having being blessed with a beautiful home and a wonderful husband. She had everything that she wanted. But, she knew this was reality and not a fairy tale.

A little time had passed and Joey's clinic was going quite well. Betsy had a lot of people coming to her to help them with their children to ride a horse. When most of the children knew it was Betsy that owned the horseback riding school they were all so eagered to go to her school. They had heard hoe good she was with horses and that she was a champion at the age of sixteen. They couldn't wait to meet her. Although there wasn't a chance that Betsy could have any children of her own she loved everyone elses children. Betsy still entered contests and won most of them. It was a passion that she had. Just riding Blazing Snow in the contests and even if she didn't win all the time it was just a thrill riding her again.

The Nationals were in town again and Betsy entered and Joey and her mom were so happy for her. Betsy was so excited it was the first time she entered in the Nationals since she was sixteen.

She knew that she might not win but she didn't mind that she was doing it for fun. The day had finally arrived and Betsy was grooming Blazing Snow. Her coat was beautiful and still glistened in the sunlight. The announcer announced that it was Betsy's turn to ride. Betsy was very excited and Joey gave her a kiss for good luck. Betsy got up on Blazing Snow and rode to the starting line.

Everyone cheered has Betsy approached the starting line. The announcer told Betsy to get ready and all of a sudden the gun went off. Blazing Snow knew just what to do. All the jumps were going just fine at first but when they came to the watering hole Blazing Snow slipped on the rail and Betsy went flying to the ground. Joey and the paramedics came running to Betsy. Joey asked her if she was ok. Betsy told him that she couldn't feel her legs.

Joey was so worried he started to cry. Betsy told him that she was going to be just fine. Her mother came and held Joey while the paramedics were tending to Betsy. They put her unto a board and carried her to the ambulance. Her mother followed them to the hospital. Joey went with Betsy in the ambulance. Blazing Snow was just fine so one of the ranch hands took her home. When they arrived at the hospital the doctor checked Betsy out. The doctor asked her if she had any feelings in her legs and she told him that she couldn't feel anything.

The doctors took Betsy for tests and they told Joey that they would take good care of her. It seemed liked forever for Betsy to have her tests done.

Finally she was wheeled back into her room. Betsy was really quiet when they put her into her bed.

The nurse told them that it will take a little time for the test to come back. So all they could do was wait. Betsy's mom had just come into the room.

She went to Betsy's bedside and told her that she was there for her. Betsy looked at Joey and she seemed a little worried. Joey touched her leg and she began to cry because she couldn't feel his touch. Joey told her that he was there for her and that he wasn't going anywhere. It wasn't long before the doctor came back with the test results.

He looked a little worried. When he got to her bedside he told her that he had good news and bad news. Betsy told him that she wanted the good news first because she knew what the bad news was going to be. The doctor told them that he was looking in her file and it said that Betsy couldn't conceive any children but that wasn't true. The doctor told them that they were expecting a baby in about six months because she was three months pregnant. He told her that she was very lucky that she didn't lose the baby with the massive fall she received. Betsy and Joey were so happy. They couldn't believe it, they were going to be parents.

Something that they wanted and didn't think they were going to get. Betsy told the doctors she knew what the bad news was. Before the doctor could say anything she blurted out that she wasn't going to walk anymore. And that she was going to be in a wheelchair for the rest of her life. Joey asked the doctor if she was right and he said yes. And that he was very sorry. He told them that Betsy had to take it easy for awhile for the baby. Betsy told Joey that he didn't have to stay with her. He told her to stop talking silly and that he was never going to leave her for he loved her so much and their child. Betsy told Joey and her mother that she was going to be just fine because she had to think of her baby. She said that wasn't going to worry about it now. Joey told her that they would take it one day at a time.

Betsy was feeling a little tired. She dosed of to sleep and she looked really peaceful.

The day had finally arrived for her to go home.

Betsy's mom bought her a motorized wheelchair.

Betsy didn't seem to mind being in the chair because she was used to it now. All she wanted was yo get home and see her horse. Betsy didn't blame her for the accident. She told Joey that the accident happened for a reason. Betsy went around and thanked all the doctors and nurses for all they did for her. Betsy felt relieved when she reached the ranch. Just the beauty of the place made her feel good inside. Joey helped Betsy out of the car. A ranch hand welcomed her back home.

He had Blazing Snow with him. Her horse looked at her with a strange look in her eyes. She guessed her horse wondered why she was sitting in a chair instead of standing. Betsy gave her horse a kiss and hug and told her that she loved her. Betsy asked the ranch hand to carry her horse into the fields and let her run. Betsy and Joey went inside she wanted to sit on her very own sofa with her husband. Joey helped her out of her chair and sat down on the sofa beside her. He started to rub her belly. They were so happy that they were going to have a baby. Everyday Betsy got bigger and bigger and Joey loved every minute of it. He told her all the time how beautiful she looked. The day had finally arrived for the baby to be born. They were so thrilled. Joey and her mom carried her to the hospital. As soon as they arrived they carried her straight to the delivery room. Joey went with her while her mother waited in the family room. She was so happy that she was going to be a grandmother. It wasn't long before Joey came up the hallway full of smiles. He was so happy he told Elaine that Betsy had just given birth to a beautiful girl. Joey told her that she looked just like Betsy.

Elaine was so happy she asked Joey what they were naming her. He told her that Betsy would tell her when they get in the room. Joey and Elaine went to her room and waited for Betsy. They brought Betsy back to her room and she had the new baby with her. Elaine started to cry when she saw her granddaughter. Betsy asked her mother if she wanted to hold her. She said that she would be thrilled to hold her. Betsy and Joey told her that they were going to name her after her adopted mother Isabella. Betsy asked her mom if she would mind. Her mom told her that it was just fine and that her sister would have been so proud to have the baby named after her. Betsy told Joey and her mother that God gave her all her blessings for a reason. Letting her have a baby with the love of her life Joey was the best blessing of all. Finding her mother was a blessing as well. Knowing through it all and having her accident well that was a blessing as well. She was told by the doctors that the accident may have happened at anytime because her spinal cord was wearing away so that is what caused the fall when her horse made the jump.

And the greatest blessing of all for everyone was their sweet Isabella. For having her was nothing but a miracle.

Printed in the United States
By Bookmasters